Our Little Hawaiian Cousin

Mary Hazelton Blanchard Wade

Copyright © 2023 Culturea Editions
Text and cover : © public domain
Edition : Culturea (Hérault, 34)
Contact : infos@culturea.fr
Print in Germany by Books on Demand
Design and layout : Derek Murphy
Layout : Reedsy (https://reedsy.com/)
ISBN : 9791041826124
Légal deposit : July 2023
All rights reserved

Our Little Hawaiian Cousin

CHAPTER I

A HAPPY CHILD

Little Auwae is beautiful; but, better than that, much better, she has no thought of it herself.

She sits in front of her low cottage home singing a soft sweet song, weaving a garland of scarlet flowers to adorn her head. As she carefully places each bud on the string, she looks up at the American flag floating in the breezes not far away.

The schoolmaster of the village tells her it is in honour of George Washington, the greatest man of the United States; that if he had not lived, America would not be what she is to-day, and she might not have been able to give Hawaii the help needed when trouble came.

But what cares little Auwae for all this? What difference does it make to her that her island home, the land of beauty and of flowers, is under American rule? To be sure, a few of the "grown-ups" in the place look sober for a moment when they speak of the change since the old days of Hawaii's kings; but the sadness passes in a moment, and the gentle, happy child-people turn again to their joys and sports.

Auwae has shining brown eyes, and, as she smiles at the homely little dog curled up at her side, one can see two rows of beautiful white teeth. Her skin, although of such a dark brown, is so clear and lustrous one cannot help admiring it. The girl is not afraid of tan or freckles. She rarely wears any head covering save a garland of flowers, if that c ould be called such; but she bathes herself frequently with coconut oil, which makes the skin soft and shiny.

She takes an abundance of exercise in the open air; she swims like the fabled mermaid; she rides for miles at a time over the rough mountain passes on the back of her favourite horse. It is no wonder that this plump little maiden of ten years is the picture of health and grace.

Her home is a perfect bower. It stands in a grove of tall cocoa-palms, whose beauty cannot be imagined by those who live in the temperate lands and who see them growing only in the hothouses. They are tall and stately, yet graceful as the willow; their long, curved stems reach up sixty, seventy, sometimes even one hundred feet toward the sky, then spread out into a magnificent plume of leaves from twelve to twenty feet in length. The breeze makes low, sweet music as it moves gently across the tree-tops and keeps company with Auwae's song.

hut with woman walking by "IT IS A LOW BUILDING WHOSE SIDES AND HIGH SLOPING ROOF ARE THATCHED WITH GRASSES"
Beneath the trees the grass is of the most vivid green, mixed with delicate ferns; the garden in front of the house is filled with gorgeous flowering plants,—roses, lilies, oleanders, geraniums, tuberoses, scenting the air with their perfume; besides many others known only in tropical lands.

The garden wall at the side is hidden by masses of the night-blooming cereus, which is such a curiosity in our own country that often many people gather to watch the opening of a single flower.

Vines hanging full of the scarlet passion-flower drape the veranda on which Auwae sits. When she has finished her wreath, she crowns her long hair with it, and turns to go into the house.

She makes a pretty picture, the little girl with her simple white dress, beneath which the bare brown feet are seen,—those feet which have never yet been pressed out of shape by stiff, tight casings of leather.

I call it a house, yet many speak of it as a hut. It is a low building whose sides and high sloping roof are thatched with grasses. Few such are made nowadays in Hawaii, for the people are fast following the example of the white settlers, and now build their cottages of wood, and divide them into rooms, so that they look like the homes commonly found in New England villages.

Auwae's father, however, clings to the old fashions of his people, and his little daughter has always lived in this beautiful grass house. The frame was made of bamboo poles fastened together by ropes of palm-leaf fibres. Days were spent in gathering the grasses for thatching the sides and roof of the house. They were woven into beautiful patterns for the roof. It was necessary to choose skilful w orkmen who knew just how to finish the corners, for the heavy rains of the tropics must not be given a chance to soak through the outside and make it damp within. When it was finished the house looked like a large bird's nest upside down.

Strange as it may seem, there is no floor in the house, but the ground is paved with stones. It is nearly covered with large mats. Some of these are made with rushes, while others have been woven from leaves of the pandanus-tree. They are stained in bright colours and odd patterns. A large screen of woven pandanus leaves divides the sleeping portion from the rest of the house.

There is no furniture, unless one can call by such a name the great number of mats in the corner. They serve for couches, bedspreads, and screens. In one corner is a collection of gourds and bowls, or calabashes, as they are called. Some of them are polished highly and prettily ornamented. If Auwae's father desired to do so, he could sell these calabashes to the American "curio" collector for a goodly sum of money; but he will not part with a single one. They are of all sizes, from that of a tiny teacup to the great "company" calabash, which holds at least ten gallons.

When there are many visitors at Auwae's home, this calabash is used at meal-time. It will hold enough food to satisfy the appetites of a large party.

The greatest treasure stands at one side near the wall. It looks like a mammoth dust-brush, but it is a sacred thing in this Hawaiian family. It is the mark of chieftainship. None other than a chief had, in the old days, a right to own such a thing, under the penalty of death. The long handle of polished bone is topped by a large plume of peacock feathers. The ancient kings of Hawaii were always attended by bearers carrying "Kahilis," as the people call them, and two enormous plumes stood at the threshold of their homes. No common person could pass by this sign of royalty or chieftainship, and enter a dwelling so marked, unless he were bidden.

CHAPTER II

AN OUTDOOR KITCHEN

Auwae does not linger within the house, but follows a sound of talking and laughter in the grove behind the house. There she finds her mother and grandmother, together with a number of the neighbouring women. They, too, are weaving garlands, for they wish to decorate their husbands when they come home to dinner.

Auwae's mother is making her wreath of bright orange-coloured seeds taken from the fruit of the pandanus. She wears a garland like Auwae's, except that she has used flowers of another colour. She has wound a beautiful vine around her waist and throat, which sets off her loose red dress to perfection. She is a fat woman, but as beauty is often measured by size among the Hawaiians, she must be considere d quite handsome.

What is it that makes her look so different from her white sisters? It is not the brown skin, bare feet, and flowing hair like her daughter's. It must be her happiness and the grace of all her movements. She seems to be actually without a care as she leans back in the grass and pats her little daughter's head. Her laugh is just as joyous as Auwae's. Her hands do not bear the marks of labour, but are soft and dimpled as a child's.

She, a grown woman, is idly making wreaths in company with her neighbours, instead of cooking and sweeping, dusting and sewing for the family! Think of it and wonder. But then, you say, this is a holiday; why should they not be idle and gay? The fact is, all days are like this to the Hawaiian mother, who lives the life of a grown-up child. The world does not seem so serious as some people think. It is a happy dream, and mother and child and neighbour dance and sing, swim and ride, in sunshine and in rain alike.

This reminds me that in their language there is no word for weather. It is continual summer there unless one climb high up on the mountainsides; and as for rain, it does not worry the people, for can they not dry themselves in the clear air that follows? There is, therefore, no need of this disagreeable word which one hears so often in some parts of America. All days are alike to the Hawaiians.

Auwae's mother has no servant, for there is little housework to be done in her home. The grass hut is scarcely used except for sleeping purposes. Both cooking and eating are done out-of-doors. The little girl's father has built an oven in the ground near the house, with enough room in it to roast the food for his own family as well as two or three of his neighbours.

people sitting on ground under palm trees by a big pot "THE PARTY SIT ON THE GRASS IN A CIRCLE"
He dug a pit in the ground and lined it with stones. Whenever cooking needs to be done, he fills this pit full of wood, which he sets on fire. When the stones are sufficiently heated, the pig, chickens, or beef, and the taro, or sweet potatoes, are wrapped up in leaves and placed in the oven; a little water is thrown over them so they will steam. Then the hole is covered over tightly, and the food is slowly and nicely baked.

Auwae's dinner has been cooking all the morning, and it is nearly time for it to be served. What do you think shall be done to prepare for it? Who of the company will stop her chattering and garland-making long enough to set the table?

As among the brown people of Borneo, there is nothing to do except to uncover the oven, take out the food, and place it on the grassy table-cloth, while Auwae runs into the house for some calabashes. There must be a large one to hold the "poi," and a smaller one for drinking-water. No plates are needed.

For to-day's dinner there is a roast of beef to eat with the poi, and delicious cocoanut milk takes the place of the coffee sometimes drunk. For dessert there are the most delicious wild strawberries, which ripen all the year round in this favoured island of the Pacific.

If Auwae wished, she could have a banana or a fresh pineapple, but she is easily satisfied. Think of it! there are forty different fruits growing near her house. One can easily understand how there is little work in providing food, and how little cooking is needed to keep the body in good health.

And now Auwae's father and several other men join the women. The garlands of flowers are placed around their necks and on their heads, and the party sit on the grass in a circle around the bowl of steaming poi.

But how do they eat? The poi, a sticky paste, is the principal dish. Surely something must be used to carry it to the mouth. That is true, and the fingers serve this very purpose. One after another, or all together, however it may happen, the company dip into the great calabash and skilfully roll balls of the paste on their forefingers, bringing it to their mouths without dropping a particle. Poi is called "one-finger," "two-finger," or "three-finger," according to the thickness of the paste.

But what is poi? is asked. It is the food best liked by the Hawaiian, and takes the place of the bread of the white people. It is either pink or lavender in colour. In the old days, pink poi was a royal dish, as it was only made for kings and queens. The different kinds are all made from the root of the taro plant. A small patch of this very valuable plant will supply a large family with all th e food they really need for a whole year.

The principal work of the little girl's father is to tend his taro patch and keep each little hillock surrounded by water. From the time of planting until the ripening of the beet-like bulbs, he watches it with the most loving care. When fully ripe, he pulls up the plants and bakes the bulbs in his underground oven.

When they have been sufficiently dried, he prepares for his most difficult task by stripping himself of his cotton shirt and trousers. You remember that the climate here is a warm one, and when the man is working hard he suffers much from the heat.

He now takes the baked taro and puts it on a wooden platter and beats it with a heavy stone pestle. From time to time he dips his hands into water as they grow sticky from handling the pasty mass. After he has pounded it for a long time, he puts it into calabashes, adds water, and sets it a way for several days to ferment.

He grows very tired before his work is over, but does it gladly, rather than do without his favourite food. It would not suit us, I fear, as it tastes very much like sour buckwheat paste. In Hawaii white people often eat the taro root sliced and boiled or baked, but they seldom touch it when prepared in the native fashion.

Now let us return to Auwae's dinner-table. The food is quickly eaten, after which the little girl passes a calabash of water around among the company. It is to serve as a finger-bowl. Does this surprise you? Ah! but you must remember these Hawaiians ate with their fingers. These same fingers are now sticky with poi, and as the people are natural lovers of water, they are fond of having every part of their bodies spotless.

A pipe and tobacco are pa ssed around for a smoke. These people, so cleanly in some other ways, do not object to using the one pipe in common. The women put away the food, and the company prepare for a picnic at the shore but a short distance from the house. They will spend the afternoon in surf-bathing, and all of them will perform feats in the water that would astonish the best swimmers in other countries.

CHAPTER III

SURF-RIDING

Auwae has a loved playmate, Upa, a boy a little older than herself. He goes with the party to the beach. Carrying their surf-boards under their arms, the two children hurry ahead to the beach of shining white coral sand. Look! The broad Pacific now stretches out before their eyes. How blue are the waters, reaching out in the distance till they seem to meet a sky just as blue and clear of a passing cloud! How the hot sunshine beats down upon the sand! Yet Auwae does not seem to mind it. She stoops to pick a wild morning-glory growing almost at the water's edge, and then dances about, saying to Upa:

"Hurrah! The waves are just fine to-day for bathing, aren't they?"

We almost hold our breath at the thought of these children trusting themselves out in the high waves rushing in from the coral reef a quarter of a mile outside. Then, too, we know there are sharks in these waters; and what a terrible death would be Auwae's if one of these creatures should grind her between his many teeth!

As to the sharks, we need not fear, as they never venture nearer than the coral reefs, which seem to be a wall beyond which they dare not pass. And as for the water! why, when we have once seen Auwae swim, we can no longer fear for her safety. It seems as though water, instead of land, must be her natural abiding-place.

But now the rest of the party have arrived, bringing with them their surf-boards, or wave-sliding-boards, as we might call them.

For those living on Hawaii's shore, much of the pleasure of life depends on these pieces of wood so carefully prepared. They are made from the strong, tough trunk of the breadfruit-tree, are highly polished, and about two feet wide. They look very much like coffin lids, and are long enough for one to stretch at length upon them.

It takes but a few moments to remove their clothing and put on their bathing-costumes. For the men, it is the malo, a piece of cloth wound about the loins and between the legs, and, before the white people came, the only garment worn by them at any time.

All are now ready for the sport. They wade out into deep water with the surf-boards under their arms. Then, pushing them in front, they swim out till they reach the breakers, when they suddenly dive and disappear from view.

There is no sign of them for several moments. Now look far out and you can see their black heads bobbing about in the smooth water beyond the waves. Watch them carefully as they wait for that great roller about to turn toward the shore. The y leap upon its crest, lying flat upon their boards, and are borne to the beach with the speed of the wind.

It must be grand sport, once they know just how and when to take advantage of the incoming wave, as well as the still greater skill in riding on that wave without being swallowed by it. It is harder to succeed than one imagines before trying the experiment himself, for the swimmers are obliged to use their hands and feet constantly to keep themselves in place.

Some of them do not even rest on the shore before swimming out for another wave slide; and as the afternoon passes they rival each other in more and more daring feats. See those two men no longer lying flat on their boards as they rush onward in the water! They only kneel, and wave their arms and shout in glee to their companions. But most daring of all is Auwae's father, who act ually stands erect as he is borne toward the shore on the crest of a huge wave. He travels at a rate sufficient to deprive one of breath.

The kind man takes time during the afternoon to give Auwae lessons in riding her own board, which he has lately made for her. Up to this time she has had to be content with swimming only, and in this, as I told you, she is already wonderfully skilful and graceful.

The hours pass only too quickly, and night suddenly shuts down upon the happy people. The moon comes out in such beauty as is seen only in the tropics. It bathes sea and shore in a soft, sweet light, so pleasant after the dazzling brightness of the sun. Auwae and Upa once more lead the party as they wander slowly homeward and again enter the shadow of the tall palm-trees.

The children look toward the mountains behind the village reac hing up so grandly till their tops are lost in the clouds, and Upa says:

"Auwae, do you know that my father is going to Kilauea next week, and he says
I may go with him. Ask your father if you may go, too. It will be such fun!"

Auwae has wished a long, long time for such a chance as this. She claps her
hands in delight, as she feels quite sure of her parents' consent.

Kilauea! She has heard so much about the mighty crater. Even now she can
see a faint reddish gleam light up the sky in the distance. The largest active
volcano in the world is showing that it is still alive and using the mighty forces
directed from the very bowels of the earth.

It would almost seem as if Auwae would feel fear at living in the shadow of a
volcano. Is she not sometimes awakened in the night by the low rumbling
sound coming to her through the clear air? And does she not then lie trembling
at the thought that she may sometime be swallowed up in a tremendous flow of
lava? Other children in towns like hers have met such a fate in the years that
are gone. Why should she not fear?

But Auwae was born here, and has always lived where she could see the light
from that huge furnace of Nature. She is so used to it that she does not dread
its power. She lives in the joy of the present, and does not consider that which
might possibly come to her.

Think of it! This home of hers and its sister islands are the children of
volcanoes, for they were born of fierce explosions of lava, thrown above the
surrounding waters from the floor of the sea. Foot by foot Hawaii has been built
up out of the water. Layer after layer of lava has been poured, one above the
other; then, cooling and crumbling, a soil has been formed on which the
beautiful plants and trees of the tropics have taken root.

But this is not the whole story of the island, for tiny creatures of the sea have
given what was in their power. The coral reefs lying along the shore have been
built up by the growth of millions of polyps, and the shining white sand is
composed of finely ground coral, which once formed the skeletons of similar
polyps.

What curious helpers Mother Nature sometimes chooses! Think of the coral
polyps and their strange lives, leaving when they die a foundation upon which

men and animals shall afterward have a home! Upa often dives for the sprays of coral, pink or white. He sells them to the white people in the village, who send them as curiosities to other countries.

Auwae and Upa bid each other good night at the garden wall. The little girl stops for a moment at the pond in the garden where many goldfish are moving about in the moonlight. She loves her beautiful fish; she feeds them every day, and often thinks how kind her father was to make the pond for her delight.

CHAPTER IV

QUARTERLY REVIEW

As she stands beside the beautiful clear water, an unpleasant thought comes into her mind. It was only yesterday that some white travellers came through the village on horseback. A little girl about Auwae's own age was in the party. She was very pretty. Her cheeks were pink and white; her hair was like the golden sunlight; her eyes were as clear and blue as the waters surrounding the beautiful island.

"Why wasn't I made white?" the little brown girl said to herself. "If I should bathe myself over and over again, it would make no" difference. I should never look like her. Oh, dear, I will ask mother why God made us so different.

She ran quickly back down the pathway till she met her mother.

"Mamma," she whispered, "I think you are just lovely as you are, but still I do wish I had been born to look like the little American girl I saw yesterday on horseback."

"My dear one," answered her mother, "God is love, and all are alike to Him. In the fields around us He has made flowers of many kinds and colours. Some roses are red, and some are white, yet the red and the white are equally admired. So it is with the people who share His life. Some are of one colour, some another; they are all needed to give variety and beauty to the world. All are equally His work. Be happy and contented, my darling, and think no more about it."

Auwae's eyes grow bright again as her mother speaks. The shadow passes away, and she is her own joyous self again.

"Of course it is all right. I'm glad I'm just what I am," she exclaims. "And yet, mamma, when Christmas comes, I believe I should like a white doll that would look like that little girl. I could have such fun playing with her and curling her hair. You know we often put red and white roses in the same bowl, and they look very pretty together."

"All right, I will remember your wish when the time comes," laughs her good-natured mother, while Auwae hastens away, half dancing, half running.

She must certainly hurry to bed now, for to-morrow is a school day, and she wishes to wake early in the morning. The moon shines so brightly to-night that Auwae can easily see to undress by it and stretch upon the floor the strip of tapa which serves for her bed. If it were dark, however, she would use an odd candle that she herself made. It is formed of candlenuts strung together. They grew near Auwae's home, and are so much like wax they burn readily. I should much prefer them to a calabash of beef fat with a rag for a wick, which is sometimes used by Auwae's mother.

"Now I lay me down to sleep," repeats the gentle child, as she kneels in her little corner, and is soon fast asleep.

Where did Auwae learn this prayer? It was in the white church in the village. There the old Hawaiian minister tells his little flock every Sunday of the One True God, and of the loving Friend who said: "Suffer little children to come unto me, and forbid them not, for of such is the kingdom of heaven."

Auwae loves her Sunday school; she delights in the music of the organ and the songs she learns there. Every three months there is a grand celebration in the church. It is called "Quarterly Review." All the children in the country for miles around come flocking into Auwae's village. It is such a pretty sight, as the boys and girls come marching over the hillsides! The girls are dressed in white, and everybody wears a wreath and festoons of bright flowers. Sometimes they sing as they march along.

By ten o'clock in the morning the church is closely packed and the music begins. There is song after song, after which the children are called one by one to the platform to speak pieces and recite Bible verses. The ones who have learned most receive the prizes. Auwae won a prize at the last quarterly review. It is a picture of the infant Jesus giving water to his cousin John from a shell. No doubt you have seen a copy of it. Auwae thinks it is a lovely picture. It is the only one of any kind in her house.

The quarterly review lasts the whole day. The children do not get tired, however. They have a picnic dinner under the trees behind the church; then they are ready for more songs, and speak more pieces, until the round red sun in the west says:

Tiki inside door with two children peeping in "AUWAE AND UPA DARED TO PEEP INSIDE"

"Come, my little ones, hurry homeward quickly. Many of you have miles of walking before you, and I cannot show you the way much longer."

Then Auwae bids her friends good-bye. She will not again see some of them till three months more have passed.

Aloha! Aloha! echoes back from the hill-tops, and our little girl turns again to her own lovely nest under the palm-trees. How different everything is now from the old days of Auwae's people! Her grandmother has told her about the hideous idols they used to worship.

There is an old heathen temple but a few miles from her home, and once, just once, Auwae and Upa dared to peep inside; then they ran away with all their might, for fear that somehow those long rows of ugly figures might become alive and follow them.

Think of it! less than a hundred years ago not only animals, but human beings, little children even, were sacrificed to hideous wooden and stone idols.

The people were in constant terror of the god of the shark, the goddess of the volcano, and other fearful beings who were ever ready, as they thought, to bring destruction upon them. Besides these, there were great giants and monsters whose anger must be satisfied by offerings of animals and men.

"How glad I am that I live now instead of a hundred years ago," says Auwae to Upa many times, as she thinks of Pele, the goddess of the volcano Kilauea. "Grandma has told me of her own mother, who really believed that Pele lived far down in the fiery crater, that she was the ruler and queen of fire. She thought that other spirits, too, lived there. There was the spirit of steam, the spirit of the thunderbolt, the spirit of strength, and I don't know how many other terrible beings. And oh, what times those spirits had together in the flames, dancing and making merry! But if the people forgot to bring Pele their offerings of hogs and bananas and all sorts of presents, she would get fearfully angry, and roar and threaten to overflow the country with lava. They would get very much frightened, and hasten to the summit of the volcano with the best they had."

And then perhaps Upa answers, "Please don't speak of those awful days any more. I like best to think of the time when our people turned from such ideas of their own accord, saying they were just nonsense. But, really, it must have taken a brave woman to do what Queen Kapiolani did. You know she walked right up the side of the mountain with her trembling followers, and kept on till she reached the very mouth of the crater, and then dared Pele to do her worst. She turned to her followers, and said: 'I do not believe in Pele! If there is no such being, no harm will come.' Of course, the people expected the fiery waves to leap up and swallow them, but nothing did happen, you know.

"Hurrah for the old queen's pluck, I say. After that, women dared to eat bananas and do many other things the priests had forbidden to all but men, saying it would make the gods angry. How silly the people used to be in those days!"

Then both children are still for a moment as they think lovingly of the good missionaries who came to their land just as their own people had given up idols. The good men and women came to tell them something better than they had ever known,—something to drive fear from their hearts, to destroy the cruel power of the priests, and to bring freedom of mind and body. What was it? The love of God!

CHAPTER V

AUWAE'S SCHOOL

On the morning after the picnic the little brown maiden is awake bright and early. After her breakfast of poi and yams she weaves a wreath of fresh flowers for her head, and, taking her books under her arm, begins her walk to the village school. Her way leads past Upa's home, and the boy is already waiting for her. As she comes near he shouts:

"Oh, Auwae, I have something to show you. You've got time to stop a few minutes without being late to school. Come with me."

And the boy leads the way down a path to a tree covered with vines trailing from the topmost branches to the ground. It makes a perfect bower of the sweet-smelling blossoms; but it is not this Upa wishes to show. He leads Auwae close to the trunk of the tree and bids her look straight upward to an odd nest gnawed in the trunk far above them. From the hole two bright eyes are peering down at the children. They belong to a large rat that has made his home in the tree; perhaps he did this to be sure of safety from small boys. Or possibly it was to secure himself from the raids of the mongoose, so common in Hawaii nowadays.

woman washing in stream "A LITTLE STREAM WHERE TWO WOMEN ARE WASHING"
"Poor little fellow," says Auwae, "I don't blame him. Father says that a good many rats live in the trees near here, but I never saw them there before. And father says, too, that the white men brought the mongoose here from India to drive out the rats, but the little fellows are not satisfied with killing them off; they want our chickens, too. It's a perfect shame. I wish they had stayed in their own country."

As the children now hurry on their way, they areobliged to cross a little stream where two women are washing. There are neither tubs, scrubbing-boards, nor soap to be seen. The clothing is dipped into the soft water and the parts most soiled are rubbed on flat stones. It must be rather hard on garments made of fine cloth, and it seems as though the women would get tired bending down. After all, there are but few things to wash, and, as the people do not work hard, their clothing cannot get badly soiled.

18

But look! Here come some of Auwae's schoolmates to join them. They are swimming down the stream. Each carries her clothing in a small bundle in her hand; she holds it out of the water as she paddles along. It is such a common matter that Auwae is not in the least surprised.

The schoolhouse is soon reached. It has but one large room, as there are but thirty children in the village. Much of the time the gentle schoolmaster sits with his pupils under the large tree near by. Auwae likes that much the best. She can never get used to the close air inside the house. But to-day the children must do some writing, so they sit at their desks and compose letters to their adopted brothers and sisters in America.

How odd it seems to see the schoolmaster tend his baby while he teaches the children! Why didn't he leave it with his wife at home? Because in this island of flowers it is the duty of men as well as women to act as nurses. It seems a strange idea to us, but, if they are satisfied, it must be all right.

Look at the baby! He is wrapped in enough clothing for six such tiny beings, and drops of perspiration are running down his face; but he does not cry.

"Aloha!" says our little Auwae, as she bows before her teacher. And "Aloha!" he replies, in a kind sweet voice. How many things this one word means! It answers for "good morning," "good-bye," "love," "thanks," and I don't know what else. But the smile that goes with it seems always to explain its meaning and make it the most delightful of words.

In Auwae's land the language was never written until the white people came to teach and help the Hawaiians. But it is very easy to understand, and Auwae could read when she had been at school only a few weeks. She had only twelve letters to learn. Every word and syllable of the Hawaiian language ends in vowels, and there are no hard sounds to pronounce. The sentences flow like music; so it is no wonder that Auwae composes poems so easily. They are very pretty, however, and her teacher is proud of her.

Auwae can tell you a great deal of the history of her island home. There are some parts of it that she loves to hear over and over again. On many a warm night as she lies on the grass with her head in her father's lap, she will look up into his kind eyes, and say:

"Papa, do tell me again about the very first Hawaiians. How did people come to live here after the island had grown up out of the sea? I can seem to see the seeds and twigs floating on to the shores with the tide. I can see the seeds sprouting and shooting up into tall trees out of the lava soil. But I wish you would describe again the boats loaded with people coming here from far away."

Then Auwae's father tells her of the time when there were no grass houses, nor brown children playing about them. He relates the stories handed down for hundreds of years about people living on distant islands across the equator. They were not treated kindly in their own land, and wished to find a new home where they could be happy and free. They were much like the Pilgrims who left Europe, and were willing to bear hardship and danger in New England.

CHAPTER VI

LONG AGO

The old Hawaiians, who in those far-away times called themselves Savaiians, loaded their boats with provisions and other needed supplies. They set sail with their wives and children in hope of soon finding a pleasant home in some new island. Their voyage was longer, however, than they expected. Storms arose, and many of the poor little children grew sick and died. But the boats, which were hardly more than large canoes lashed together, rode safely onward. After many days the people saw the shores of the Hawaiian Islands ahead of them.

How glad they were to stand on dry land once more! They found a sheltered valley where they soon made themselves comfortable. They had brought with them some chickens, two or three pigs and dogs, besides the seeds of the breadfruit, and the kou trees. They found the taro plant already growing there. They had made poi from it in their old home, so they knew how to use it. Besides this, they found the kapa-tree. From its bark they could make new garments to take the place of their sea-worn clothing.

They were very happy. Children were born in this new and beautiful land. Seeds were planted; more pigs and chickens were raised. It was the Golden Age of Hawaii, for there were peace and plenty.

Even the Brownies helped the settlers, and often worked wonders in the land. At least, this is what Auwae's father said, and I think he believed in these queer little beings.

When he mentioned the Brownies,—Menehunes he called them,—Auwae's eyes grew large with delight. She loved to hear about this race of dwarfs who were said to have built immense fish-ponds and sea-wells. Why, if you yourself, should doubt there were such beings, Auwae could point to their large stone ruins not far from her home. She would say:

"Do you suppose any living people could set such great stones in place? Surely not! The Brownies are the only ones having strength enough to do work like that. Why, they are able to pass big stones from one to another for miles."

Her father tells her that the secret of the Brownies' power is that they work together and work till their work is done. When human people sleep they are busy, but if mortals walk abroad at such times the Brownies make themselves invisible. Those were certainly wonderful times when the spirits of the earth worked for men, and did such mighty deeds in Hawaii.

But an end soon came to this joy and comfort, for men began to quarrel and have wars against each other. Then the Brownies withdrew their aid, and left them to themselves. Sickness fell upon the Hawaiians. There were many rulers, each one trying to gain all the power possible. The rich grew richer, and the poor poorer. Wicked priests, as well as the chiefs and masters, held the people in fear. It was a sad, sad time. The "chiefesses" (for there were women rulers) were no better than the men.

At last a child was born in Hawaii, who was unusually strong and wise. He grew up and became a great chief. His name was Kamehameha. That word means "The Lonely One." He was very ambitious. He looked over the island of Hawaii, and said to himself:

"I will make myself king of this whole land. I will bring the people more closely together. I will change many of the customs which are bad and harmful."

He kept his word. He rallied his own men around him, and was soon ruler of the entire island. But still he was not satisfied. He looked across the sea to other islands, and said:

"I will be ruler over all these, too. My kingdom shall be a powerful one."

He sailed with his troops in his strong war-canoes, and soon landed on the island of Maui, not far from Hawaii.

The king of that island had been warned of the coming of the enemy. He was already marching down a narrow pass between the mountains to meet The Lonely One and his army.

Kamehameha did not waste a moment. He rushed up the pass, his men following him in single file, and there, in a narrow pathway at least a thousand feet above a deep abyss, the two armies met. As each one of the Hawaiian soldiers stepped upward, he met and grappled with one of the enemy. One or the other was sure to be hurled downward over the precipice, and meet death below, if he were not already killed on the narrow pathway.

It was a terrible battle. When night came the army of Maui was no more, and Kamehameha was ruler of that island.

He was suddenly called back to his own home, for news came that a rebel leader in Hawaii had risen against him. This leader encamped with his men near the volcano Kilauea. As the great Kamehameha advanced to meet them an earthquake shook the land; a violent storm of cinders and sand rose out of the crater to a great height, and then fell down over the mountainside.

When the men were able to advance once more it was found that a large part of the rebel army had been killed by the eruption. At this the people exclaimed:

"Surely the Goddess Pele was angry at the rebel chief. She chose this way to show her favour toward Kamehameha."

After this there were other troubles, but The Lonely One grew more and more powerful. At last he became the ruler of all the islands. He did with them as he had promised himself, and the people were united and happy as long as he lived.

CHAPTER VII

THE COMING OF THE WHITE MEN

At nearly the same time that this brown king was born in Hawaii, a baby was born in far-distant England, who was, many years after, the first white person to visit Auwae's home. This baby's name was James Cook. He was a little country boy. His father was very poor. James might not even have had a chance to learn his letters if it had not been for the kindness of a good woman who lived in his village.

The boy had to work hard, even when very small. He did not like his work, either, and after awhile he said:

"Oh, how I long to leave this place and be free! I would rather live on the beautiful blue ocean than here in the country. I shouldn't mind doing the hardest things on board a ship."

After awhile he made up his mind that he could not bear it any longer. One dark night he packed up a small bundle of clothing and ran away to sea.

Do you imagine he found a kind captain waiting at some dock who became his good friend and helper? Don't imagine it for a moment. He did find a captain, and a ship, too. He also got a chance to work as a cabin-boy, but he was badly treated, and had to work far harder than he ever did on land.

Yet he loved the life of the ocean so much that he kept on sailing, and worked his way up to a high position. He even became a captain. People now called him "Captain Cook," and he was sent on long and dangerous voyages in the English navy. When he was at home in England he was invited to great dinners, and given high honours, for he had become a famous man.

At last he was asked to make a more dangerous voyage than he had ever yet tried. Wise men thought there might be a short way for ships to sail from Europe to Asia by going north of America. There were many icebergs, to be sure, as well as seas all frozen over, but perhaps there was a warm current running through the ocean. Captain Cook was so wise and brave he was the very man to try to find the Northwest Passage, as it was called.

He started out with a goodly fleet. He sailed for many weeks. Many strange things happened. You must read the whole story of the voyage some time. But the brave captain did not find the Northwest Passage; he did, however, discover the islands of Auwae's people.

One morning at sunrise, as he came sailing into one of the harbours, the brown natives flocked to the shore. They had never seen a ship before. They wondered what it could be. Was it a forest that had slid down into the sea? Or was it the temple of Lono with ladders reaching up to the altars?

It seems that Lono was one of the gods in whom the brown people still believed. He had gone away from their island long before, and had promised to come back some day on an island bearing cocoanut-trees, swine, and dogs.

They thought the tall masts must be the cocoanut-trees, and when they saw the dogs and swine on board the ships, they were quite sure the promise had come true. Captain Cook himself must be Lono come again, and the sailors were lower gods who served him.

One of the priests brought a red cloak and placed it on Captain Cook's shoulders. This was the mark of his greatness. Such an honour could only be offered a god.

There were great feasts for the visitors. Offerings of fruit, chickens, and all good things possible were made to the white men. They grew fat on the fine living. They were merry over their good times. No doubt they laughed at the foolish belief of the savages, as they called them. But they did not say:

"My brown friends, we are glad you are so kind to us, but please don't think we are great beings. We are human beings like yourselves."

Do you not think that would have been wiser and more honest?

After awhile one of the sailors died. Then the brown people began to think. They said among themselves:

"Gods cannot die. These people die, so they cannot be gods."

They began to watch more closely. Captain Cook was very quick-tempered. He and his men sometimes quarrelled with the natives and were cruel. At last, sad to say, the brave captain was killed in one of these quarrels.

Some people believe the Hawaiians of that time were cannibals and ate his dead body. But this is not true. Auwae would feel very badly if she thought her American brothers and sisters could believe this. Captain Cook was a very great and brave man in the opinion of the brown child, as well as in yours. But he ought not to have let the people believe he was anything else than himself,— a white traveller from other lands.

There is a monument to his memory on the island, and when you visit Auwae she will take you to see it.

After Captain Cook's death other white men came and taught the Hawaiians many things. They helped the rulers in governing wisely; and at last the people saw it was best to put themselves under the care of their white brothers.

Auwae likes to read about the old days, however. She delights in hearing her grandmother tell of her own youth; of the visit the king once made to her village; and of the grand celebration in his honour. The days were given up to feasting and entertainments. Men practised boxing and wrestling for a long time beforehand; there were wonderful feats on horseback, in which Auwae's grandfather took part.

As he rode at full gallop through the village, he surpassed all others in leaning from his horse and picking small coins from the ground. Best of all, the old woman said, as he rode along he wrung off the necks of fowls whose bodies were buried in the ground. And this he did without checking his horse's pace at all.

But the most joyful part of the day was when the king, fairly covered with wreaths of flowers, took his place under a beautiful pandanus-tree; then his subjects, one by one, came up before him, and, cheering and bowing, gave him offerings. It was always the best which the people offered their lord. There were presents of live fowls, hogs, clusters of bananas, cakes of seaweed, eggs, cocoanuts, nets of sweet potatoes, taro; everything which the king could desire.

"What joy and good-will those days brought!" says Auwae's grandmother. "It was the happiest time of my life."

The old woman takes a great deal of interest in everything her little granddaughter does. She is very proud of Auwae's collection of land-shells. She thinks it must be the finest one any child possesses in the whole island. She, herself, gave Auwae at least half of the different varieties. She had kept them from the time of her own childhood.

Did you ever hear of land-shells? They are found on the low, overhanging branches of trees, and the little creatures who make their homes in them would die if you were to put them into the salt water. They are very tiny, and are of many different tints. Auwae has beautiful blue ones, as well as rosy pink, pale yellow, green, violet, and I don't know how many other colours. In little basket trays, side by side, they look very pretty. Each variety has a tray of its own.

Many days must have been spent in gathering the collection; many different people have helped Auwae in making it,—for often only a single kind of shell can be found in one whole island. People in Hawaii exchange specimens, just as the American boys and girls trade postage-stamps with each other. The white people in the village would like to buy Auwae's collection to send to a museum across the ocean, but she would not think of parting with it.

CHAPTER VIII

THE DIVER

When school is over, Upa and Auwae go home through the woods so that they can throw stones in a certain waterfall. They have no fear that snakes will suddenly take them by surprise, for there is not a single one in the whole island. Neither do they hear frogs croaking beside a shady pool, for neither frogs nor toads have ever hopped upon Hawaiian soil.

Wherever they come to an open space beneath the trees, they play ball. Upa made his own ball out of leaves which he packed closely together, and Auwae bound it with sweet-smelling grasses when he had pressed it into shape.

The boy's busy mind has planned new sport for the afternoon, and he says:

"Auwae, after you have had your nap, do you want to fish? Old Hiko is going out to the coral reefs, and he has promised I should go with him. He says I may bring you, too, if you wish."

Auwae claps her hands with pleasure, for it will be a great treat. Hiko is the only one in the village now who dives for fish. The other men use lines made from the fibres of the flax-plant, and are satisfied to sit in their boats, and lazily wait for bites. Auwae has grown to be a fine diver, and hopes to learn something by watching the old man.

After a dinner of dried devil-fish and sweet potatoes, with baked seaweed for a relish, and a delicious pudding of grated taro and cocoanut milk, our little brown cousin stretches herself under the trees, and is soon fast asleep.

She is dreaming of catching fresh-water shrimps in the stream near her house when she is roused by a gentle pat on her forehead. It is Upa, who says:

"We must hurry, Auwae. Hiko is going in half an hour, and he will not wait for us."

Auwae is instantly wide awake, and after a loving "Aloha!" to her mother, she hurries to the shore with Upa.

The old fisherman is already there in his long, clumsy-looking canoe. He hollowed it from the trunk of a tree, and there is just room enough inside for himself and the two children. At one side of the boat there is an outrigger to balance it, and make it quite safe.

Hiko has a queer-looking paddle in his hand, and another beside him. These paddles are like clumsy wooden spoons; it seems wonderful how fast they can make the boat travel over the water.

The children wade out from the shore to the deeper water where the boat is riding; then with a bound they spring into their places, Auwae to steer, and Upa to seize the other paddle.

On they go till they are directly over the coral reef. The sea is a beautiful green, and as clear as glass. Now they let the boat float along, and all eyes are bent down upon the groves of coral below the water. All at once Hiko rises suddenly to his feet, and springs upon the edge of the canoe; but first he seizes in one hand a small fish-net, and in the other a palm leaf.

Ah! down he dives, straight over the side of the boat! Down! down! Will he ever come back? Do not fear. This is mere sport for him,—surprising a shoal of fish at play among the coral spires. To the waiting children it seems as though he were gone a long time, but in reality it is no more than a minute.

As he appears again out of the water they shout in excitement, "What luck, Hiko? What luck?" But they do not need to ask, for they see that his net is half-full. He has actually brushed the fish into it with his palm leaf, as your mother brushes crumbs from the table into the tray.

How beautiful are these fish! They are of many colours: red, green, blue, and yellow. Among them is one of a delicate pink tint, shaped much like a trout. Still another is a queer-looking fish with a purple body, a blue spotted tail, and a dark head that shines brightly in the sunlight.

But the greatest treasure in the old man's collection is the sea-cock, or ki-hi ki-hi, as he calls it. Its back is covered with stripes of black and yellow; it is perfectly round in shape, while a long, transparent ribbon is fastened to its nose.

Hiko lifts the sea-cock from the net with great pride. To show the children how beautiful it is while floating in the water, he fastens a cord through the creature's head, and drops it below the surface. It looks now like a gorgeous butterfly as it trails after the boat.

But Hiko is not satisfied yet. He says he will dive once more, as he wishes to give Upa's mother a goodly mess of fish for her supper. At the next dive he is gone for a longer time than before. Auwae grows fearful just as his old face appears once more. He is puffing hard for breath, and his eyes are red and blood-shot. He has been even more successful this time, but is quite tired. He tells the children they can allow the boat to float for awhile. They may rest for a luncheon on some of the dainties he has just secured. Each may choose the fish liked best.

It seems queer to see the pleasure with which Auwae's pearly teeth meet in the tail of the sea-cock. But such is the habit of her people, and raw fish seems no stranger food to her than fresh-picked strawberries or pineapples.

boats in the surf "IT IS LIKE A LONG, GRAND TOBOGGAN SLIDE"
The party now paddle their way homewards. But, listen! A sound of music comes from the direction of the shore. See! there are at least four canoes filled with people. They are coming out for a race, and, as they move along, are merrily singing in rhythm with the motion of their paddles.

As they come nearer, our little brown maiden sees her father and mother amongst the party. She stands up in the canoe, and shouts: "Oh, mamma! we have had such fun! Hiko says we may stay out and race with you, too."

And now Hiko turns the canoe in the direction all the others are going. The surf is running high; there is a good breeze blowing toward shore, so there will be fine sport. All who hold paddles work with a will, and the canoes are soon beyond the breakers; then they line up and watch for a big roller.

They have only a minute to wait; all eyes turn as Hiko shouts, "Hoi! hoi!" ("paddle with all your might").

The canoes rush onward with all the force the rowers can put into them; for the boats must be moving fast enough when the breaker reaches them to keep up with the onrushing water. Otherwise they will be overturned, and the people obliged to swim ashore; which would certainly not be pleasant.

Hurrah! The canoes are suddenly lifted up to a great height by the mighty power of the roller; then down they suddenly drop to level water again and speed onward to the shore. It is like a long, grand toboggan slide, only it is on water instead of snow or ice.

Auwae's boat reaches the beach first of all. There is a shout of laughter from the gay company who follow. It is because one of the canoes has been left far behind the others. Of course the best fun lies in winning this queer water race.

The sport continues for an hour or more, till it seems as though every one must be tired out. Then they draw the canoes up on the shore and lie about on the sand for story telling.

CHAPTER IX

STORIES OF OLDEN TIME

Auwae's father repeats a legend handed down through generations of his family. "More than four hundred years ago," he says, "not far from this very spot, there lived a great chief. His home was not Hawaii, but he came from a distant land to fight and win honour under the king of this island. He became powerful, and was much loved by the people. His relatives followed, and settled here with him, and all went merry.

"The time for the monthly festival drew near; games, races, and trials of strength were planned to make a pleasant holiday for all. The chief himself was to take part. He and his dearest friend were both well trained in sliding down the steep hillsides on their polished sledges; so they agreed to vie with each other at the festival to see who could win.

"How seldom, friends, these sledges are used now! What a grand sport it was! I have a sledge at home used by my father, not more than six inches wide, and at least eight feet long. The runners are finely curved and polished. You must all have seen it.

"But to come back to my story. The chief knew well just how to throw himself upon the sledge; he knew the difficult art of keeping his sledge under him as he slid down the steep race track; he was able to guide his sledge with the greatest skill.

"But his friend was as skilful as himself, so the people expected a close contest. Many wagers of bunches of bananas and fat pigs were made.

"The time came, and the two men went up the hillside with their sledges under their arms. They laughed and chatted, and had just reached the top when a beautiful young woman suddenly appeared before them.

"She bowed before the chief, and said, 'Will you try the race with me instead of your friend?'

"'What!' he exclaimed, 'with a woman?'

"'What difference should that make, if she is greater and more skilful than you?' was her answer.

"The chief was angered, but he only replied, 'Then take my friend's sledge and make ready.'

"And so these two, the chief and the strange, beautiful woman, rushed down the hillside. For a single moment she lost her balance, and the chief reached the goal first.

"How the people cheered and shouted! But the woman silently pointed toward the top, as much as to say, 'Let us have one more trial.'

"Again the chief climbed the hillside, this time with the woman by his side. As they were about to start once more, the stranger exclaimed:

"'Your sledge is better than mine; if you wish to be just, you will exchange yours for mine.'

"'Why should I?' answered the chief. 'I do not know you. You are not a sister or wife of mine.' And he turned without further heed and flung himself down the steep descent, supposing the woman was also on the way.

"But not so! She stamped her foot upon the ground, and suddenly a stream of burning lava poured forth and rushed down the hillside. The chief reached the foot of the hill and turned to see the fiery torrent destroying everything in its way.

"Too late, he understood everything now. The strange woman was none other than the goddess Pele, who had taken this form to sport with men. He had angered her, and she was about to destroy him and all his people.

"And look! There rode the goddess, herself, on the crest of the foremost wave of lava. What should he do? He instantly turned aside and fled with his friend to a small hill from which he could see the awful death of his people.

"And now the valleys were filled with the burning torrent. Pele did not intend to let him escape. Nothing was left but the ocean. He reached it just as his brother drew near in his canoe. Together they fled to their old home across the waters, and never again dared to visit Hawaii, lest the dreadful goddess should come forth against him."

When the story is finished, tales are told of the old days of war and bloodshed; when the word of the chief was law to his people; when no life was safe from the power of the priests and chiefs. Then, indeed, were surely needed the cities of refuge still standing on this island.

"It is at least a hundred years ago," says old Hiko, "that my grandfather fled to the Pahonua, that strong old city whose walls have sheltered many an innocent man and helpless woman. He was accused of breaking the 'tabu' the chief of his village had laid upon a certain spring of water." (Of course, as you know, "tabu" means sacred, and so the water of that spring must not be used by any one except the chief himself.)

"My grandfather was then a young man, gay and happy. He would never have dared to break the tabu, but an enemy accused him of so doing, and the chief sent armed men to kill him. A good friend heard of it in time to warn him, and he fled over the mountains on his trusty horse.

"His pursuers were in full view when he reached the entrance to the city of refuge. Here they believed he was under the protection of the gods, so they turned back. Drawing a long breath of relief, he entered the city. He lived for some days in one of the houses built inside its massive walls. Then he came home again without fear, for he could never more be harmed for the deed of which he had been accused.

"In those times, my children," says the old man, "the thief, even the murderer, was pardoned, once he reached the city of refuge. And during wars it was the place to which women and children fled; there alone were they safe."

But the people are rested now, and do not care to think longer of the olden times. As the tide is far out, a dance upon the beach is proposed. Upa pounds his drum, and another of the party plays upon a bamboo flute. All the others move about on the coral sand in slow, graceful circles.

 While they are enjoying themselves in this way, we can examine Upa's drum. He made it from the hollow trunk of a cocoa-palm. It is covered with shark's skin. Odd as it seems to us, it serves his purpose very well, and the boy keeps good time with the dancers. While he beats upon it he delights in watching Auwae move about on the sand. She is the very picture of grace and happiness.

CHAPTER X

UP THE MOUNTAIN

The pleasant days pass by for Auwae and Upa, and the time comes for the great trip to Kilauea. You must understand that Kilauea is not the volcano itself, but the largest crater on the side of Mauna Loa. Many grown people as well as children picture a volcano as a great cone with only one deep pit, down into which they can look when they reach the summit.

This is not always so; for the fire raging in the heart of Mauna Loa has burst out in more than one place on its sides. Kilauea is the largest of these outlets, or craters. It is a hard journey to climb even so far as this. Very few people are daring enough to go still farther and journey to the summit of Mauna Loa.

Auwae's mother actually grows excited while she gets her little daughter ready for the trip. She does not care to go herself.

"It is too much work. I know I should get tired; but you can tell me all about it, my child, when you come back. Then I can see it through your eyes. And Upa's father will be kind, and will take good care of you. I shall not worry."

When the first light of the morning shines through the tree tops, three clumsy-looking horses stand in front of Auwae's door. Upa and his father use two of them; the third one is for our little brown maiden, who appears with a fresh garland of flowers upon her head and a smile on her red lips.

She springs upon the saddle without help, and sits astride of the horse just as Upa does. In fact, all Hawaiians ride in this way, and it is very wise. The women could not travel safely over the rough mountain passes if they rode like their white cousins.

"Aloha! Aloha! Aloha!" echoes through the grove, and the party is soon out of sight. They have more than thirty miles of climbing before them; the horses must walk nearly all the way, as it is a steady rise from the village to the edge of the great crater.

At first, the way is through a perfect forest of breadfruit, candlenut, and palm trees. Among them are ferns growing from twenty to thirty feet high! Their great stalks are covered with a silky, golden-brown fibre. Other ferns, more delicate, are wound around these and live upon their life.

It is cool in the shade of the trees; the way is narrow and the horses must go in single file to keep out of the thick underbrush. Presently the way grows lighter and the party come out of the forest and pass a large sugar plantation. Chinese labourers are cutting down the long canes and carrying them to the mill to be crushed. The white overseers are hurrying from one place to another, urging on the men and giving directions, while through it all Auwae can hear the rush and roar of a waterfall. She cannot see it, because the mill and boiler-house hide it from her sight.

The party move to one side to let a team of mules pass them on the narrow road. The mules are laden with kegs of sugar which must be carried to the coast and shipped to distant lands.

The children would like to stop awhile on the plantation, but Upa's father says they must not delay. It will be evening before they can reach the volcano-house.

As they climb higher and higher up the mountainside, the air grows cooler, yet the heat from the sun is so great they are still too warm for comfort. Suddenly a heavy shower takes them by surprise, and Auwae cries out in delight:

"Upa, isn't this fun? I'm going to open my mouth and let the raindrops fall right in. I'm so thirsty! Aren't you?"

The children lie back in their saddles and leave their trusty horses to follow their leader onward and ever upward. No one gives a thought to wet clothing, for will it not be dry again a few minutes after the rain stops falling?

See! the lava-beds stretch out before them. It is clear enough now that Hawaii, the island of flowers, was born of fire. All these miles of gray, shining substance once poured, a broad river of fire, from the crater above. Some of the lava looks like broad waves; again, it is in pools, or rivers, or coils, with great caves here and there. These caves are really bubbles which have suddenly burst as they cooled.

Auwae looks off to each side of the road, built with so much labour up the mountain; then she thinks of what her grandmother has told her of her own journey to Kilauea, years ago. At that time there was no road over the lava-beds, and her horse slipped many times as he stepped on places smooth as glass. And many times his hoofs were badly cut on sharp edges, and left bloody marks behind him.

The air is quite still. Not a sound can be heard. No birds nor insects make their homes on these lava stretches. Yet do not think for a moment that nothing grows here. The moist air and the rains have been great workers, and, in some strange way, delicate ferns, nasturtiums, guavas, and even trees, have taken root, so that the lava-beds are nearly covered.

Hour after hour passes by. Auwae gets so tired she nearly falls from her horse. The luncheon has been eaten long ago. There is no water to drink except what the showers have left in little hollows by the wayside. The children have stopped their chatter and lie with closed eyes on their horses' backs. The smell of sulphur grows strong, and Upa's father turns around to call out:

"Children, here we are at last! And there is my old friend Lono in the doorway to welcome us."

CHAPTER XI

THE VOLCANO

Auwae suddenly forgets the long and tiresome ride, as she jumps from her horse's back in front of the hotel. This hotel is built on the edge of a crater! Think of the family who live here year after year! Night after night they look from the windows upon the raging fire below, yet are not afraid. Many a time the earth shakes beneath them, and the house rocks to and fro. The shelf of lava on which it stands may break at any moment, and the people within may suddenly be flung over the precipice. Yet they live on, and work and play as others do who have nothing to fear.

In many places around the house are cracks in the earth from which sulphur fumes are rising. As the children look out in front they see the crater itself, more than nine miles round, and nearly a quarter of a mile deep.

As they creep out and look over the edge, what is before them? The crater is filled with steam, while over in a distant corner of the pit they look for the first time upon the "house of everlasting fire," as the old legends call it,—the home of the goddess Pele.

The flames rise and fall, now high enough to light up the evening sky, now low as though dying out, and with it can be heard the breathing of this great furnace of nature. It sounds like the restless ocean many miles away.

Auwae and Upa hold each other's hands tightly and do not speak. Surely this is a wonderful sight. They will not forget it as long as they live.

 They are so tired, however, that they are soon fast asleep in "white people's beds," as they call them. They do not awake till the sun has driven away the clouds which hang about the place in the early hours of morning. Upa's father has already eaten breakfast and attended to his business with the landlord.

He tells the children that horses are at the door to carry them down into the crater; for they have begged him to let them see everything possible.

What a ride this is down the rough, jagged side of the pit! The horses pick their way step by step over the sharp broken lava. But even here beautiful things are growing. There are delicate ferns, silvery grasses, pink, white, and brilliant blue berries. It seems as though Mother Nature wished to hide the frightful masses of black and gray lava.

Now the air gets very hot; steam and sulphur pour through great cracks in the floor of the crater; the lava itself will burn if Auwae dares to touch it with her fingers.

The floor of the crater, looking quite even from above, is broken up into hills and valleys, immense ridges and rivers of lava which have poured forth, one above the other, at different times.

After two hours of hard riding and walking, Auwae and Upa reach the lake of living fire and look down, down, into its depths. But they cannot see the bottom. Each throws in a garland of flowers as an offering to the goddess Pele. They know she does not exist, but it is an old, old custom of the people, and they have not quite grown out of the idea that it is safest to do so.

For, look at the flames leaping up at this very moment! "People may be mistaken," thinks Auwae, "and the goddess may get angry if we are not polite, and suddenly drown us in fire!"

 It is dinner-time before the party get back to the hotel. They are willing to rest all the afternoon under the tree-ferns near the house. They lazily pick the ohele berries growing about them, as they tell the village news to the landlord's family.

On the evening of the third day our little brown maiden finds herself safe at home once more. She is very well, but quite lame and sore from her long ride. Her mother says she shall have a lomi-lomi, and she will feel all right again.

Auwae stretches herself out on a mat while an old woman of the village pinches and pounds and kneads every part of her dear little body. Do you suppose it hurts? Just try it yourself the first time you have a chance, and when it is over see if you do not feel as limber and care-free as Auwae does.

She dances about under the trees, and exclaims: "Oh, how nice it is to be alive! What a lovely home I have! But I'm glad I've been to Kilauea, though I would not like to live there."

At this moment she sees her father coming down the path to the house. He was away when she got home, and she runs to welcome him.

"But, dear papa, what are you hiding behind you?" she cries.

"I have a present for my little daughter," he answers. "It has cost a large sum, but my only child deserves it, I well know. It is something for you to treasure all your life."

He hands her a bamboo cylinder, telling her to see what is inside. The excited girl opens one end, and out falls a band of tiny yellow feathers to be worn as a wreath. It is more precious to this Hawaiian child than a diamond ring or gold necklace could possibly be.

Why, do you ask? Because of the time and labour in getting the feathers, which are found on only one kind of bird in the islands, or any other place, for that matter. This little creature is called the oo. It lives among the mountains. Under each of its wings are a few bright yellow feathers no more than an inch long. Hunters spend their lives in snaring this bird. They place long sticks smeared with a sticky substance where the oo is apt to alight. After it is caught, the precious feathers are plucked and the bird set free.

While Auwae crowns herself with her new wreath, her father tells her that next month she shall go away with him on a steamboat. She shall visit Honolulu, the capital of the islands. There she shall see the wonderful war-cloak of Kamehameha the Great. It is made entirely of oo feathers. Nine kings lived and died, one after the other, before this priceless cloak was finished. And now it is guarded as one of the greatest treasures of the country.

Yes, Auwae shall see, not only this, but many wonders beside. She shall ride through the streets with neither man nor animal to carry her. She shall talk with people miles away by placing her mouth to a tube. She shall see how her white cousins live and dress.

But her father does not doubt that she will be glad to come home again to this little grass house with the quiet and the peace of the village life.

THE END